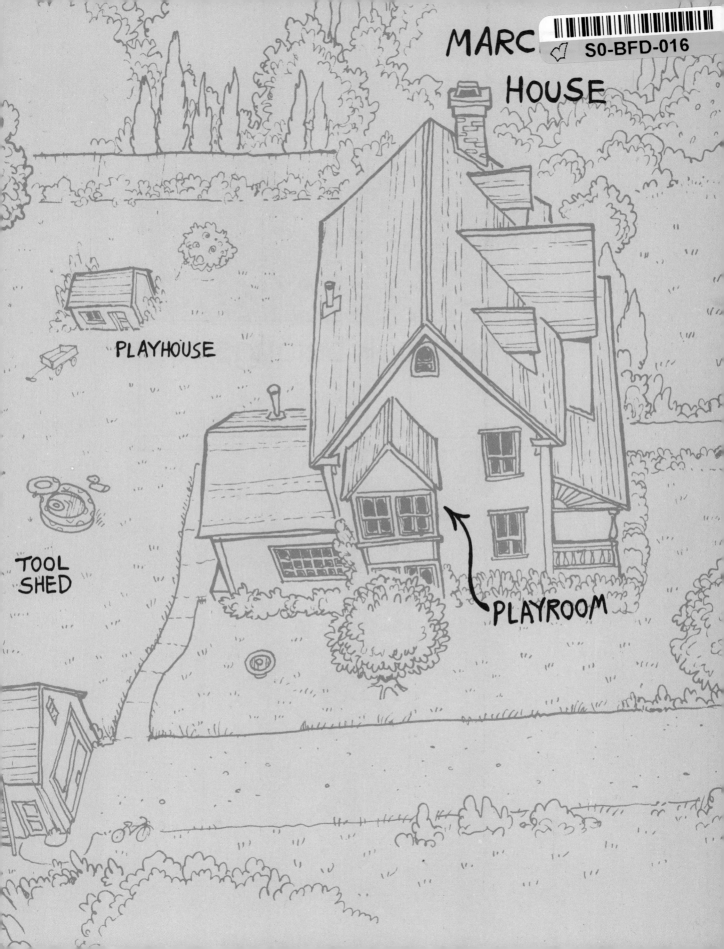

MARC'S
HOUSE

PLAYHOUSE

TOOL
SHED

PLAYROOM

This book belongs to:

_____

Raggedy Ann & Andy's

TIM'S BIG ADVENTURE

A LYNX BOOK

This book is published by Lynx Books, a division of Lynx Communications, Inc., 41 Madison Avenue, New York, New York 10010. The name ''Lynx'' together with the logotype consisting of a stylized head of a lynx is a trademark of Lynx Communications, Inc.

Raggedy Ann and Andy's Grow-and-Learn Library, the names and depictions of Raggedy Ann, Raggedy Andy and all related characters are trademarks of Macmillan, Inc.

"I can't wait to go outside today," said Raggedy Andy.
"Me, too!" said Tim the Toy Soldier, who had looked
forward to this day all week.

Today was the day Marcella had gone with her parents to visit her cousins. Since there would be no people at home, the dolls would have a chance to go outside and play in the fresh air all by themselves.

"Let's make a fort out of the playhouse," said Tim.
"I'm going to hop around the vegetable garden," said
Sunny Bunny. "Maybe I'll meet some real bunnies to play
with."

"I'm going to pick wildflowers and make a wreath to wear in my hair," said Babette the French Doll.

"Oh, my," said Raggedy Ann, pulling back the window curtain. "Look outside."

"Oh, no!" groaned Tim, when he saw the sky full of dark, angry-looking clouds.

All of a sudden, it started to rain.

"The whole day is ruined," cried Tim.

"Now we have nothing to do," grumbled Tallyho.

"Sure we do," said Raggedy Ann, pulling a large picture book from a bookshelf. "I'll read you a story."

"Who wants to hear a dumb old story?" groaned Tim.

"I do," said Raggedy Andy, who was looking at the pictures over his sister's shoulder. "This looks like a great story! Wow! Look at that dragon!"

"I thought we were going to have fun today," Tim mumbled to himself.

"Oh!" cried Tallyho happily, when he saw which book Raggedy Ann had chosen. "I was hoping you'd read us that book someday!"

All the dolls loved to hear Raggedy Ann read from Marcella's books. She really made the stories come to life. All the dolls, except Tim, that is. Right now, Tim didn't want to listen. Even as Raggedy Ann began to read the story, he was stomping his black boots and making little noises with his toy drum. Tim huffed and puffed and refused to join the circle of dolls.

The other dolls looked at Tim. He could tell they were not happy that he was making noise.

"Once upon a time," Raggedy Ann began, "there was a land of wizards, and dragons, and flying horses."

Tim tried not to listen to Raggedy Ann. But he put down his noisy drum and was quiet. He looked around the playroom. He saw the dollhouse standing gray and dark in the corner. Then Tim looked out the window. In spite of himself, he began to listen to the sound of Raggedy Ann's voice.

"The brave young soldier tiptoed in carefully, for he knew that a dragon was near . . ."

Raggedy Ann's voice seemed to be fading far, far away. Tim looked out of the playroom window and stared at a big gray cloud. A bright streak of lightning flashed across it.

All of a sudden Tim blinked—the lightning had turned into fire, and the cloud he was watching became a huge purple dragon!

The dragon stood right before Tim's eyes. The dragon was angry. Before Tim could decide what to do, he heard Babette cry out.

"Help! Help!" she shouted. A mean-looking wizard was dragging her into what looked like a castle.

Tim decided to make a run for the castle gate.
The dragon decided to make a run for Tim.

As Tim reached the gate, it began to creak up . . . higher and higher and higher.

"I have to save Babette!" Tim thought.

He grabbed the edge of the gate, but it didn't stop.

Tim swung into the air over the moat.

The dragon kept coming.

But the dragon, so excited about chasing the soldier, forgot something important.

Splash! Into the moat went the dragon. The dragon forgot that he couldn't swim.

Plop! Into the water Tim fell, because he was laughing so hard at the dragon that he forgot to hold on.

"Hissssss!" went all the dragon's fire, as it turned into steam. Tim could float very well in the water, so he headed toward the shore.

"Wait for me!" whined the dragon. "I can't swim!"

"Calm down," called Tim. "The water isn't deep. Why, a big dragon like you could walk right out."

And that's just what the dragon did.

Now Tim knew that the dragon wasn't scary at all. But because the dragon had chased him, Babette was a prisoner in the castle.

"Dragon," Tim called. "I've helped you. Now you must help me." He looked over at the castle walls.

"I would," the dragon answered. "But those walls are too tall for me to climb."

Suddenly the dragon called out, "Look!"

Tim turned and saw Tallyho. Tallyho had changed. He was now a beautiful horse with golden wings that helped him sail across the sky.

"I have come to fly you over the castle walls to rescue Babette," he said to Tim.

"Goodbye, Dragon!" Tim called, as Tallyho galloped with him into the clouds.

"Good luck, Soldier," the dragon called back.

Tim and Tallyho flew nearer and nearer to the dark, gray castle.

Soon they were inside the walls.
Tallyho dropped gently to the ground, and Tim climbed
off to look around. There were so many rooms with so
many windows! How would he ever find the right one?

"Here! Here I am!" Tim heard from above. His eyes followed the sound. He could see Babette waving from a window in the castle tower.

"There she is!" Tim shouted. "Let's go!"

Babette stepped away from the window and Tim crawled in.

"Are you all right?" he asked.

"Tim! I'm so glad you're here!" Babette answered. "The wizard will be back any minute. Let's get out of here!"

Just as Tallyho carried the two friends over the castle
walls, Babette looked back.

"Oh, no!" she cried.

Tim turned back and saw the wizard flying close
behind them in a bright balloon.

"What will we do?" Tim wondered.

Just then Tim looked down and saw something huge
and purple running along the ground.

"I'll help you now, Soldier!" shouted the dragon. And with one mighty huff, he blew fire at the balloon. The balloon burst. The wizard fell into the water below.

Babette and Tim clapped and cheered loudly as they watched the wizard and his balloon fall. The wizard sputtered and muttered, but brave Tim, Tallyho, and Babette were on their way home. . . .

Then Raggedy Ann read the words, "The End."

Tim blinked his eyes once. Then he blinked them again.
Could he have *imagined* that he was the brave soldier and
that Tallyho was the horse with golden wings? Did he
imagine that Babette was the beautiful princess captured by
the wizard? How could that be? For here he was right in
the playroom.

"The sun is shining now, Tim," said Raggedy Ann.
"You can finally go outside and have your adventure."

"I *did* just have an adventure," Tim said.

Raggedy Ann smiled. "When we come back in, I'll read you another story," she promised.

"Great!" said Tim. "I think I'd like to be a pirate this time."

Tim now knew that as long as he could use his imagination, a great adventure was only a storybook away.

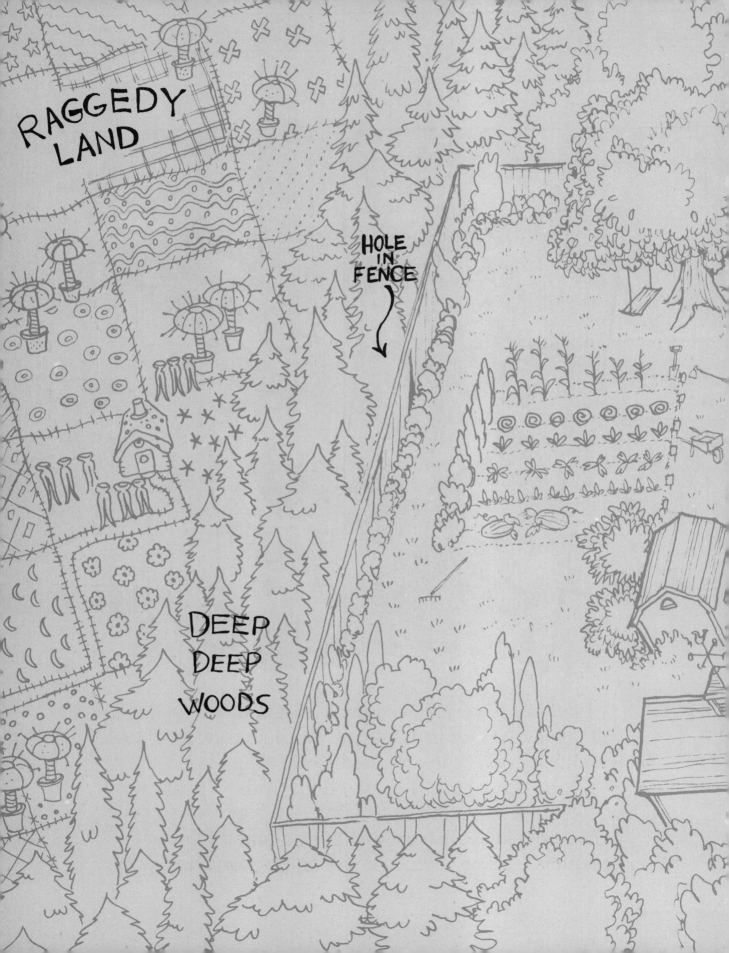